W3275s

SID SEAL,
HOUSEMAN

SID SEAL, HOUSEMAN

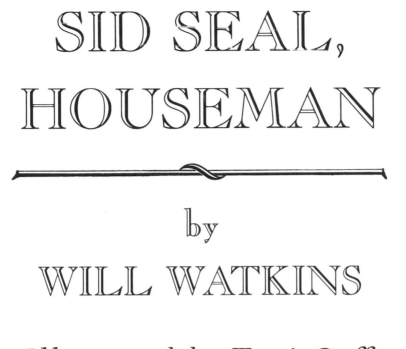

by

WILL WATKINS

Illustrated by Toni Goffe

ORCHARD BOOKS

A DIVISION OF FRANKLIN WATTS, INC.

New York

ORCHARD BOOKS
387 Park Avenue South
New York, New York 10016

ORCHARD BOOKS CANADA
20 Torbay Road
Markham, Ontario 23P 1G6

Orchard Books is a division of Franklin Watts, Inc.

Manufactured in the United States of America
Book design by Tere LoPrete

10 9 8 7 6 5 4 3 2 1

The text of this book is set in 14 pt. Baskerville
The illustrations are pen and ink.

Library of Congress Cataloging-in-Publication Data

Watkins, Will.
    Sid Seal, houseman.
    Summary: Waltham de Swine, a young pig in a rather wealthy family, finds his life much enlivened when an irrepressible seal comes to work in his home.
    [1. Seals (Animals)—Fiction. 2. Pigs—Fiction.
3. Household employees—Fiction] I. Goffe, Toni, ill.
II. Title.
PZ7. W3227Si 1989   [Fic]   88-60095
ISBN 0-531-05784-4
ISBN 0-531-08384-5 (lib. bdg.)

For Alexandra

Contents

1

An Old-Fashioned Bathtub

Mr. and Mrs. Livingston de Swine, their cook, their chauffeur, their maids, and their only son, Waltham, and his nanny all lived in a handsome town house on Beacon Hill. It was a house always pointed out to visitors because of its stately appearance and its shiny brass door knocker in the shape of a cod.

On this particular Sunday, the de Swines were spending their morning in their usual way: Livingston having a little snack before lunch, his wife, Drusilla, discussing a guest list with her husband, and Waltham reading quietly.

At least that is what he was supposed to be doing. Actually, he was sitting in an armchair near the window, watching two piglets just his age playing catch in the park. He didn't know them, but he wished he could.

Just as he was wondering if the sun would still be shining after lunch and if the boys would still be there and whether or not his mother would let him go outdoors, a loud splashing noise and a "Heave ho, my hearties" came from his parents' bathroom.

He jumped up to investigate and a moment later came flying back out of the bathroom and down the stairs.

He rushed across the waxed parquet floor and burst into the dining room out of breath. His parents

were at the long polished table. "Now, now, Wal
tham," began his mother. His father looked up from
his plate with a start.

"There's . . . there is a *seal* in your bathtub!" he
blurted out, collapsing onto a side chair.

"Well! Really, Waltham!" cried his mother in an-
noyance. "There are no seals on Beacon Hill, and
especially not in our bathtub. You are letting your
imagination run away with you again." And she
turned and picked up her guest list and began to
read with an irritated shrug.

"Papa," said Waltham, turning to his father, "won't
you come and look? He's splashing water everywhere!"

"Humor him, please, Livingston," said Waltham's
mother without looking up from her lists, "or we'll
have tears and snuffling." Livingston grunted, pushed
back his chair and followed Waltham up the stairs.

"It's true, Drusilla!" shouted Livingston moments
later, as he stood in the dining-room door. "That seal
had the nerve to tell me to 'butt out' when I opened
the bathroom door."

Drusilla sighed loudly and stood up with determi-
nation. "All right, gentlemen," she said, "show me
your seal." She followed them up the stairs, shaking
her head.

Livingston rushed ahead of her and threw open the door of the bathroom dramatically.

There in the middle of a large, old-fashioned, claw-footed bathtub sat a middle-size seal, dark gray in color and sporting a handsome set of whiskers.

"You stop poking your pink snouts in here!" he shouted in a hoarse voice. A wet sponge shot past Livingston's ear and bounced off a portrait of Great-aunt Lavinia Porker.

"What's the matter with you pigs?" asked the seal, spreading his flippers questioningly. He looked at Drusilla and Livingston. "Haven't you ever heard of

knocking?" He reached down with a flipper and released the plug.

"Hand me a towel, please, Missus," he said, looking at Drusilla. She stared at him angrily, folded her arms and looked away.

Very timidly, Waltham took a large, fluffy pink towel off a rack and, tiptoeing up to the tub, handed it to the seal.

"Thanks, mate," he said, looking at Waltham with a whiskery grin.

He stepped out onto the oval bath mat, and as he dried himself, he began singing heartily.

Pull boys, pull,
The wind's on our quarter
And the anchor needs a lift.

Livingston and Drusilla looked at each other, eyebrows raised. This seal was clearly setting a bad example for young Waltham.

"Do you really have an anchor in there?" cried Waltham, forgetting his shyness and rushing up to peer into the tub.

"That's right," said Drusilla, thrusting Waltham aside. "Up anchor and out of here!"

"What?" exclaimed the seal, heading for the bathroom door. "No clam doughnuts for breakfast? No codfish balls?"

"Down the stairs and out, seal," said Drusilla, ignoring his remark.

"This is not what you'd call pig hospitality," muttered the seal as he thumped down the stairs.

Drusilla rushed down the stairs ahead of him and flung open the heavy front door. Across the street was the greenery of a small park.

"Well," said the seal, looking up at Livingston, "aren't you going to call me a cab?"

"Stuff and nonsense," interjected Drusilla. "Out!" And she pointed down the front steps.

The seal shrugged his shoulders, barked a few times (Waltham thought maybe he was laughing), and waddled out the door.

" 'Bye, Mr. Seal," said Waltham in a small voice. He waved at him and smiled faintly.

The seal turned and looked sharply at Waltham. "Watch your heading, my lad," he said. "You're on a good course." And with a jaunty wave of a flipper, he turned and hopped down the front steps.

Drusilla closed the door behind him with a bang. "Not a word about this to the servants," said Drusilla pointedly to her husband.

"Certainly not, certainly not," he said soothingly as they reentered the dining room.

Waltham stood quietly by the front door, looking through the sidelight. He saw the seal enter the street, hail a cab, and clamber in. He watched until the cab turned the corner and disappeared from view, leaving Pinckney Street empty and silent. Even the two piglets were gone.

2

A Seal Is Hired

The Friday following what Waltham privately called Seal Day instead of Sunday, the de Swines were giving a very important dinner party for the Forbes-Hampshires. Drusilla carefully planned every detail, but a few hours before the event, disaster struck.

Waltham and Livingston came home from the museum to find Drusilla shrieking into the telephone, "But I need her tonight, not next week," and she banged down the phone.

"Parlor Maid had a fight with Cook; she left bag and baggage an hour ago without even making a scene. We're expecting some important guests in an hour."

"Now, now, I'm sure we can get by without a maid," said Livingston soothingly.

"Get by!" thundered Drusilla. "I will not 'get by' in my own house. I'm sure if I telephone around energetically I can turn up a maid. This dinner is the social event of the year." And she turned and strode huffily up the stairs.

Her husband followed her offering vague encouragement. "Well, yes, well, yes," he kept saying.

Waltham climbed up the stairs behind his father very slowly. When his parents disagreed, he always felt sad and a little teary. He had started toward his

favorite hiding place in the nursery when he heard Drusilla angrily exclaim, "How did you get in here again, you silly seal?" Her voice echoed in the bathroom as she stood in the doorway.

"That's for me to know and you to find out," said the seal. He sang lustily and poured Drusilla's best purple bath salts into the water around him.

> *Haul away, my lads,*
> *Haul away,*
> *Haul away, Hispañola*
> *Haul away.*

With every "haul away" the seal would shake more salts into the water.

"Using my salts!" exclaimed Drusilla. "What nerve!" She stalked up to the tub menacingly.

"Come on, Missus," said the seal, "give me a break."

"Oh no, not that seal again," said Livingston. He rushed into the bathroom and collapsed on the hamper.

Waltham walked up to the tub. "Hi, Mr. Seal," he said shyly.

The seal cocked his head at Waltham and winked.

"Oh dear," said Livingston, "this is the limit; not only do we lose a serving maid but this peculiar seal turns up in our bathtub again. I'm afraid people will talk about us for all the wrong reasons."

"You need someone to wait on table?" asked the seal, suddenly popping his nose over the top of the tub. "I used to be a waiter in a ritzy Singapore night-club."

"I'm going to the phone for a maid to serve tonight," said Drusilla, ignoring the offer. "And I expect you to remove yourself from my tub promptly," she added, looking hard at the seal. "You know your way out."

While Drusilla shouted on the telephone, Living-ston remained seated on the hamper in the bathroom. He kept tactfully trying to hurry the seal through his bath.

Waltham, overcoming his usual shyness, was trying to find out how the seal had got into the house. "Did you come through the back door, then?" he asked.

"The secret, kid," said the seal, bending toward him and speaking behind his flipper, "is to have a good compass and a following wind."

"Oh," said Waltham, confused but too polite to admit that he didn't understand.

"No one, absolutely no one, is available on such short notice," said Drusilla.

"Lady, you're letting in a northeast blow," said the

seal. Waltham, who only five minutes before had felt like crying, started to giggle.

"Why don't we call off this dinner, Drusilla?" asked Livingston with a sigh. "I know it's going to turn into a nightmare." Drusilla shot her husband and her giggling son a furious glance and marched up to the bathtub.

"Did you say you were a waiter?" asked Drusilla, staring uncertainly at the seal.

The seal sat up suddenly in the tub, one flipper resting on the edge, whiskers gleaming. "Missus," he said, "you should see me with a napkin over one flipper and a plate on my nose."

"Nose!" exclaimed Drusilla with a start, not at all sure that was suitable.

But Waltham loved the idea: a seal with Mother's best dishes balanced on his nose would be too exciting to miss. He had to say something. "Think of it, Mother. People would be talking about your dinner for years to come."

"That will be enough," said Drusilla, looking sternly at Waltham.

Waltham gulped and looked at the floor.

The seal looked at Waltham, then at Drusilla, "Trust a seal, Missus," he said softly.

Drusilla knew that the situation was desperate. She

drew a sharp breath and decided to suspend her suspicions about the seal's abilities as a waiter.

"Report to the kitchen at six," she said briskly, adjusting the long strands of pearls around her neck.

"Aye, aye, Missus," said the seal as he heaved himself out of the tub.

Livingston took him into his dressing room and fitted him with a black bow tie.

The seal, who had introduced himself as Sid, looked in the mirror. He brushed back his whiskers with both flippers. "What do you think, kid?" asked Sid, turning to Waltham, who had been standing in the doorway.

"Well, I think you look just like a waiter," said Waltham.

"Thanks, pal," said Sid with an amused snort, and he took another quick look in the mirror.

That evening, at the Forbes-Hampshire dinner party, the politely chattering guests fell silent when Sid bounced through the swinging kitchen door with a tray of shrimp cocktails balanced on his nose.

Livingston smiled nervously; Drusilla stirred uncomfortably in her chair.

Waltham, who was not invited to dinner parties with grown-ups, had persuaded his nanny to let him take an early bath, and while she thought he was viewing an educational television show before bed, he had sneaked out of the nursery and hidden on the upper stairs, where he could see the entire dining room through the banisters.

Sid proved to be an able waiter. He would set the tray down beside each guest and, much to Waltham's delight, gently nudge off the plate with his nose.

Mr. Forbes-Hampshire was greatly impressed. "Not everyone has a seal who is willing to wait on table. Where did you find him, Livingston—been lurking around the aquarium?" He threw back his head and let out a hearty laugh.

Livingston didn't want to say "We found him in our bathtub" to such an important guest, so he smiled mysteriously and didn't answer Mr. Forbes-Hampshire.

From his perch on the stairs Waltham saw that, as the dinner party progressed, Sid was beginning to get wound up. At one point he burst in with the roast on a tray, and twirled it several times on his nose while barking and clapping.

"Sidney!" cried Drusilla, exasperated. "Please don't dizzy the roast."

"Oops!" he replied. "Sorry, Missus."

Waltham, watching the revolving roast, had fallen backward on the stairs laughing. Unfortunately, his laughter attracted the attention of his nanny. She pounced on him. "This is no place for a delicate piglet," she said.

She carried him off to bed but not before he had a chance to watch Sid bring in the dessert soufflé. He was positively self-controlled and rather bossy.

"No talking!" he cried as he slipped through the door, balancing the soufflé dish with the cork pad underneath. "Sit still, folks," he added, "or the soufflé will fall flat as a flounder."

Although Drusilla was a trifle embarrassed by Sid's manner, she was also secretly delighted. Only good manners kept her from making just such bossy remarks to her guests.

Needless to say, the dinner party was an enormous success. All of the dinner guests were talking about the amazing waiter, and if phone calls between guests and the general comments in the neighborhood were any indication, he was a sensation.

A Room with Bath

Drusilla and Livingston sat over teacups a few days later and discussed the recent events. Waltham sat there too, quietly drinking a cup of cocoa. The dinner party had made the newspapers, and a photographer from the newspaper had come around hoping to photograph Sid in action.

Sid, however, had left after the party without a word. He hadn't even returned to collect his pay.

"Just when I had been thinking of hiring him as a houseman," said Drusilla unhappily. She had been highly impressed by his skill and efficiency.

"He was a bit cheeky," commented Livingston. "But I'm sure you would have polished him up," he added, smiling at his wife.

"He winked at me," said Waltham, "and he told me I was on a good course."

Livingston looked at Waltham and chuckled. Then they all fell silent. Drusilla put down her cup and sighed.

Suddenly the silence was broken by a hoarse voice drifting down from upstairs:

> *Pull boys, pull,*
> *The wind's on our quarter*
> *And the anchor needs a lift.*

"Sidney!" exclaimed Mr. and Mrs. de Swine at the same moment. All three arose and rushed upstairs asking each other questions as they clattered up.

Sure enough, there was Sid, splashing in their bathtub. He was scrubbing his back vigorously with a long-handled scrub brush.

"Hi, kids!" he said, looking over the edge of the tub at them. "Long time no see."

Drusilla cringed at this familiarity, but she quickly steeled herself. She was determined to hire Sidney immediately.

"Will you tell us," cried Livingston, running up and down the bathroom, "just how you got in here?"

He lifted the lid of the hamper and looked in, as if he expected to find another seal hidden there.

"Are you looking for my duds?" asked Sid. And he let out a rollicking series of barks.

"Nonsense," said Livingston, annoyed, "I would simply like to know how you got in here."

"Never mind that," said Drusilla, stepping up to

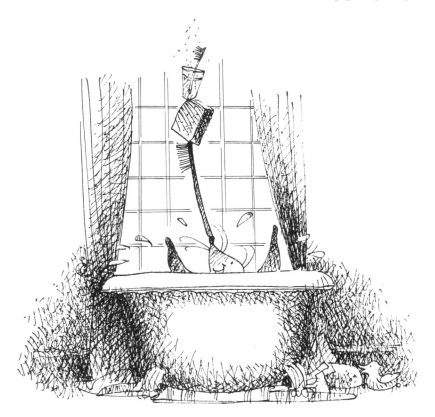

the tub. "The important thing is that you are here, so that we can offer you a permanent job as waiter and houseman."

"Does that include a room with a bath?" asked Sid.

"Oh yes," said Livingston, "we can offer you a room on the fifth floor. It has a very large old-fashioned bathtub."

"That'll do nicely, sport," said Sid. "As my Uncle Mert used to say: 'A roomy tub is the quickest way to a seal's heart.'"

"I like roomy tubs too," said Waltham. "And you want to know something? I can dive under, come up, and spout water, just like a whale."

"Hey, kid," said Sid, "I'm counting on you to show me." And he tickled Waltham under the chin and winked at Livingston.

Sid moved in that same afternoon, and when Drusilla went up to explain his duties, Waltham followed her.

Compared to the de Swines, even one as young as Waltham, Sid didn't have many worldly possessions. Inside his suitcase, lying open on the floor, were several large bath sponges, a loofah mitt, a beach ball, three toy boats, and a bath towel with the initials S.S. embroidered in the corner. There was also a large old-fashioned trunk standing in the corner, locked securely with a big brass padlock.

"Besides waiting on table," began Drusilla, "we would like you to perform various other duties around the house."

"Missus," broke in Sid enthusiastically, "I love to perform."

"I'm pleased you like to perform services," said Drusilla haltingly, "and I'm sure you will do so with dignity." She drew herself up and fixed him with a severe gaze.

"Oh yes, Missus," said Sid, "I'm sure you will enjoy my dignity—it'll be sensational!"

"Excuse me," interrupted Waltham, who couldn't contain himself. "What's in that big trunk?"

"That, my boy," said Sid, wiggling his whiskers and rolling his eyes, "contains the mysteries of Davy Jones's locker." And he gave his snorty laugh as he patted the trunk.

4

Nanny Trotter
Meets Her Match

Sid settled in quite nicely in the de Swine town house. Most of the other servants seemed to like his cheeky cheerfulness. He could make Cook laugh with his twirly enthusiastic way of waiting on table, and the parlor maid would often roll her eyes at some remark of Sid's.

Livingston enjoyed him wholeheartedly. Drusilla would have preferred greater respect, but she thought very highly of Sid's serving talents.

With Nanny Trotter, however, it was quite a different matter. From the first day, when Sid waddled into the nursery to have a visit with Waltham and to have a look at his "quarters," there was war.

The first room of the nursery that Sid popped into

was fitted out as a schoolroom. A tall, gangly pig, glasses on his snout, was sitting at a desk.

"You mean the kid's got a teacher right here at home?" exclaimed Sid. He looked around in surprise.

"Waltham tends to catch colds and earaches. He's not very strong," said the teacher. "His parents feel he should be taught at home, away from rough and naughty pigs."

"Maybe the little guy needs some excitement," said Sid. "The wind and the whitecaps, the night sky at sea, his bow lifting through a breaking swell." And he gestured enthusiastically with one flipper.

The teacher smiled weakly. "Waltham is simply too delicate," he said.

"Hmmph!" exclaimed Sid. "In a pig's eye!"

And he turned and waddled into Waltham's bedroom.

"No smelly beasts around my charge!" roared Nanny Trotter when she spotted Sid. And springing out of her rocker, she rushed at him menacingly, waving a hot-water bottle she had snatched off Waltham's bed.

Sid was momentarily startled. He retreated out the door crying, "Blimey! A monstress, a monstress!"

Hearing herself called a monstress, Nanny Trotter's

rage mounted. "Out, out, fish breath!" she squealed.

"Oh dear, oh dear," said Drusilla, who had heard the commotion. "I should have prepared Nanny for the arrival of Sidney." And she rushed into the nursery to calm her down.

"Who, madam," began Nanny Trotter, "is that slimy, bewhiskered creature?" Drusilla shut the door behind her, and their loud voices immediately became muffled.

"One thing this seal knows," said Sid to himself in the hall. "I've got to show Nanny Monstress who's boss."

Several days later, during which they elaborately ignored each other every time they met in the house, Sid decided to take matters into his own hands. At first light, he sneaked quietly into Waltham's bedroom and woke Waltham by tickling his toes with a flipper. "Hey, pal," he said, "do you want to play with my toy boats?"

"Oh yes, please," said Waltham, instantly awake. And he hopped out of bed and followed Sid out of the room.

The moment of truth came an hour later when Nanny came to wake Waltham for breakfast.

She shook the blanket-covered form gently. Quick

as lightning Sid sat up, wrapped his flippers around
Nanny and gave her a very wet, whiskery kiss.
"Mommy," he barked. "Mommy love!"

Nanny Trotter staggered back with a shudder.
"Out! Out! Vile creature!" she bellowed. Rushing out
into the hall, she began crying, to no one in particular,
"Insolence! Insolence!"

It took some time for both adult de Swines to
persuade Nanny Trotter not to leave. That done and
Waltham discovered in Sid's tub playing with the toy

boats, all three of them sat down with Sid and pleaded for an end to war.

"Yes, okay, okay," said Sid. "I'll ignore her, if she ignores me, as long as she lets me visit Wally."

And so it was agreed: both would ignore each other in the house. Nanny Trotter accordingly put her snout in the air and lowered her eyelids whenever she spotted Sid. And Sid, whenever he saw her, would put his formidable nose in the air and snuffle past Nanny, waving and wiggling his nose haughtily.

All of the servants whispered that Sid was the clear winner in the nose-in-the-air contest.

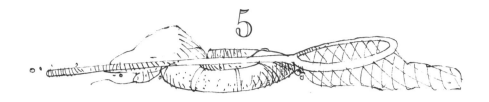

Waltham Has a
Swimming Lesson or Two

One very warm Saturday afternoon in October, when Nanny Trotter was sick in bed with a severe cold, Sid was asked to take Waltham to his swimming class at the Y. Sid cheerily accompanied him there and then sat on a bench watching Waltham learn the backstroke.

Waltham was excited to have Sid with him. "Sid, watch me!" he kept calling.

His teacher was a no-nonsense pig, very slim and self-assured in the water. He was annoyed by Waltham's constant calling out to Sid.

And as Sid watched, he became more and more restless. Finally, he began to mutter to himself. "Where's the fun?" he asked. "What about under the water—now that's real swimming!" And almost before he knew what he was doing, Sid had slipped into the water.

"Follow me, Wally," he called. And he dived, rolled in the water, and with a quick surge, zipped out onto the apron of the pool at the opposite end.

"Yea!" yelled Waltham. "That looks like fun." And he splashed enthusiastically in the water.

Waltham's teacher scowled at Sid. "Where's your suit, fella?" he asked. "This is not a skinny-dip pool."

"Suit?" asked Sid. He was genuinely surprised.

"Yes, swimming suit. You can't swim in here without one."

"Are you jealous of my sleek figure by any chance?" asked Sid. And he patted himself with his flippers. Some lady pigs in flowered bathing caps tittered loudly.

"Out of here!" shouted Waltham's teacher (who was also a lifeguard). He looked like he meant business.

Sid waddled into the ladies' locker room. "Who'll know the difference?" he said. There he found a huge basket with rental bathing suits. He quickly wiggled himself into a very large pink flowered suit. It certainly wasn't a good fit: too loose in some places, too tight in others. It was, however, a swimming suit, and Sid waddled back into the pool and splashed in.

"Come on, Wally," he called, swooshing up to Waltham, "climb on my back." Wally grabbed on with a squeal, and Sid swept off to the far end of the pool. He made great waves that spilled over the edges of the pool.

"Hey, wait a minute," yelled Waltham's teacher.

"Now take a big breath, Wally, and hold on tight. I'm going to do some real swimming." Sid made a twisting dive under water and in no time came up with a snort at the opposite end.

"Wheee!" cried Waltham after he had taken a breath.

"Here we go, dolphin-style," yelled Sid, and under they went. Sid rolled up in the middle of the pool, dove again, and in a very swift movement came up at the far end of the pool and bounced out on the apron.

Waltham stood up. "That was really fun," he said, a little breathless. "Nanny Trotter never does anything like that. She just sits and knits."

"You'll have to stop messing around," said the lifeguard, who had swum up to where they were. "You're disturbing the water."

"Is that so?" said Sid. "It seems to me that my kind

of swimming is less disturbing than your floundering around on top of the water."

"Underwater swimming isn't real swimming any- way," said the lifeguard, warming to the discussion.

"Not real swimming, mate!" exploded Sid. He dove suddenly into the water, streaking straight to the bottom and, in one tremendous leap, burst out of the water in the middle of the pool, turned a som- ersault and crashed back into the pool with a loud impact.

Great waves surged back and forth in the pool. The three ladies squealed and fled.

Sid shot out at the opposite end and onto the apron.

"That's all for you, Buster," said the lifeguard, picking up a long-handled net that was used to clean the pool. "I want you out of here."

Sid made a rude noise and dove into the water with a plop. He raced to the other end while the lifeguard ran alongside waving the net. By the time the lifeguard got to that end, Sid was almost back to the other end. Sid barked and clapped his flippers.

"Come on, pokey pig," he taunted.

Back came the guard, running, and Sid sped to the other end. Finally, the lifeguard made a misstep,

slipped, and fell into the pool. His long handled net swung around and swept the three squealing ladies back into the pool with a huge splash.

In a flash, Sid slipped out of the pool. "Come on, Wally," he said. "Time to go." And in a moment they were out of the pool and on the elevator whizzing down to the first floor.

On the street, Sid's pink swimming suit provoked some comments from passersby. "Hey, baby!" yelled a truck driver. "Show me the way to the beach."

"Who needs a pig for a father?" fired back Sid, as he hurried Waltham (who was still in his swimming suit) home.

There was a commotion when they arrived. A telephone call from the Y had preceded them. But Sid weathered the storm. Livingston came vigorously to his defense, and Waltham made a shocking scene when he thought Sid might be fired.

"Waltham!" exclaimed Drusilla. "I've never seen you behave like this. You've always been our quiet and well-behaved piglet." Nevertheless, she hastily promised that Sid would not be dismissed if he made a sincere effort to reform.

For his part, Sid promised to try to curb his impulsiveness with greater attention. And thus he remained on best behavior for a number of weeks.

Grandma at the Aquarium

One gray and rainy Sunday right after Thanksgiving, Sid asked Drusilla's permission to take Waltham with him on a visit to his grandmother. Since Waltham was standing right there nodding his head enthusiastically at his mother, there was no way she could politely refuse.

A short time later they were walking down the front steps of the house. Waltham was wearing a slicker, sou'wester, and rubber boots. Sid had borrowed a sou'wester from the chauffeur because he didn't like rain trickling in his eyes.

"Where does your grandmother live?" inquired Waltham as he walked beside Sid, holding onto his flipper.

"Oh, she's retired," said Sid. "She used to teach water ballet at the Boston Natatorium, but her arthritis got too bad."

"But where does she live?" persisted Waltham, looking up at Sid through the rain.

"She moved into the aquarium last year," said Sid.

"It was a tough decision for her. She's always been very independent."

When they arrived at the aquarium, which sat at the harbor's edge, the rain had let up. The pool where seals usually swam was empty.

"But where is she?" asked Waltham.

"Well, I guess Grandma's inside," said Sid. "I'll have to dive in and come up in the pool inside. Wait here, Wally."

He took off his sou'wester and stuck a flipper into the water. "Yow!" screamed Sid, pulling his flipper out. "I hate cold water. Give me a heated pool, please, or a cozy bathtub."

With a loud groan he dived in, disappearing into the murky water. A few moments later, he burst out of the water and hopped up on the side next to Waltham. "Brrrrrr!" he said, shaking himself all over. "She's coming in a minute." And he waddled up and down along the edge, warming himself.

With a faint splash, a rather small seal bobbed quietly to the surface. There was gray around her muzzle. "Good gracious, what a surprise," she said mildly. Her voice was thin but very clear. She had a precise way of speaking. "I've heard a great deal about you, Waltham, and it's very kind of you to come and visit me."

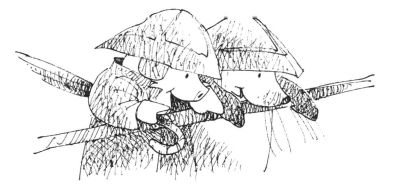

"Hi!" said Waltham, taking the flipper extended to him. "Mrs.— Mrs.—"

"Oh," she said, "Sylvia is the name I used when I taught water ballet, but you can call me Grandma."

"She's been teaching the resident seals here something of her art," said Sid. He was still shivering slightly.

"What's water ballet?" asked Waltham, looking at Grandma. He had imagined that it was something to do with squirting water to the rhythm of music, but he wasn't sure.

"Water ballet," said Grandma Sylvia dreamily, "is poetry in motion; it's a dance of body and water."

"Oh, I see," said Waltham politely, but he was still puzzled. He didn't see at all.

"You float and turn, you pivot and swish gracefully." Grandma's voice trailed off as she turned in the water. She did a slow, graceful somersault and came up with her flippers stretched out. "It's dancing in the aqueous, a rhythm of turning and rolling . . ." Her voice trailed off again, dreamily.

"Grandma!" shouted Sid, bringing his grandmother out of her reverie.

"Sorry, my dear," she said softly, "I do get carried away."

"Do you think the resident seals you've been teaching might be interested in giving us a little demonstration?" asked Sid. "I don't think Wally here gets what you're talking about."

"Oh yes, yes, splendid," said Grandma, bringing her head up out of the water. Her eyes were shining. "Just a moment." And she disappeared below the surface of the water with a mild gurgle.

After a few minutes, other seals began popping to the surface, eight in total including Grandma.

They greeted Sid and then came up to have a look

at Waltham. They began oohing and aahing. "What a darling little piglet," said one seal.

"So very grown up," said another one, as Waltham acknowledged an introduction politely.

"My mother says," said Waltham, "that I'm not a piglet; I'm a small de Swine."

All of the seals laughed, in a kind of barking chorus.

"So sweet," commented one.

"Are you ready for a demonstration?" asked Grandma. "Joe said he would put on the music in two minutes."

"Now, seals," she announced, clapping her flippers together, "remember to concentrate; let yourselves flow into the sound."

The seals quickly formed into a circle, flippers out. The slow rhythm of "Anitra's Dance," which Sid loudly announced was something by Grieg, began to come out of the loudspeakers mounted above the pool.

The seals began moving in a slow, stately circle, following the rhythm of the music. Suddenly they all streaked out from the wheeling circle and dived in unison.

When they came up, they began rolling, first one way, then another. The patterns changed like a kaleidoscope: they divided, spread out, dived, and turned, always in perfect unison.

Finally, with a concluding turn of the music, the eight seals surged out of the water and fell back with an elegant splash timed to match the final pinging of triangles at the end of the piece.

"Was that what you expected, Waltham?" asked Grandma, swimming over to him.

"It was much nicer," said Waltham. "How do you remember to do things with music?" he asked.

"That, my dear," said Sid's grandma, "is a matter of discipline and dedication to art." She gestured dreamily, touching a flipper to her breast.

"And it takes a lot of flipper grease, especially in that arctic water," chimed in Sid.

Sid's grandmother laughed merrily. "Sid has always hated cold water, but he has a wonderful sense of humor."

She turned in the water and came up closer to Waltham. "Come and see me again, Waltham. I enjoy seeing young people—sometimes it's lonely here, and the visitors are not always very polite."

Wally leaned down and kissed Sid's grandmother. He had to laugh because her whiskers tickled. Sid rushed over and gave his grandmother a snorty kiss. She laughed merrily again.

"Remember," she said, moving slowly away, "water ballet is poetry in motion—so graceful—it charms the heart." And she slowly disappeared beneath the dark, glimmering water.

They walked home silently through the empty strees; Waltham, walking close to Sid, held tightly to his flipper.

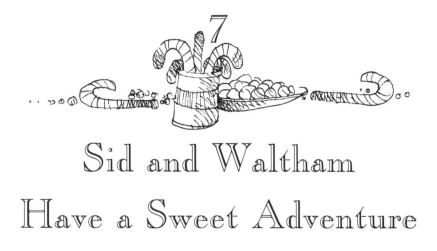

Sid and Waltham
Have a Sweet Adventure

Just after New Year's, the weather in Boston turned sharply colder, with a harsh wind gusting off the sea.

One particularly gray morning, Waltham was astonished when he peered at the barometer in his father's study. "Down, down, down!" he exclaimed.

"Good heavens," said his father, "I wonder what it means." He snapped on the TV, and they soon heard the weatherman excitedly announce that a snow hurricane was heading straight for Boston.

"A snow hurricane!" said Waltham. "I've never heard of that."

Drusilla quickly sent Cook on a shopping expedition for food and candles, while Livingston, with Sid and the chauffeur, Chester, in tow, bustled around the house taping the windows so that when the wind gusted they wouldn't fall in. They collected water in the bathtubs and brought up quantities of firewood from the basement to be prepared for any emergency.

"It's always best to anticipate trouble," Livingston told Sid, who was stacking firewood in the kitchen.

"Yes, as long as the anticipating isn't too much trouble," observed Sid dryly.

Waltham's tutor, who had to take the train in from Salem every day, had been warned not to come in to work, and by noon Waltham was very restless and out-of-sorts.

In midafternoon, as it began to snow lightly, Sid suggested to Drusilla that he should take Waltham out for a walk—just in the neighborhood.

Nanny Trotter, who had become impatient with Waltham's whining, readily agreed. "But not too far," she insisted, directing her remarks to Drusilla.

Fifteen minutes later, Waltham, all bundled up, was skipping down the street ahead of Sid. Sid himself had put on a scarf as a concession to the coming storm.

"Let's walk down to the Esplanade and visit the playground," suggested Waltham. "If you wouldn't mind, Sid."

"Swell, kid!" exclaimed Sid, who was very happy to be out of the house, too.

They walked down the hill through the lightly falling flakes of snow, crossed the footbridge over Storrow Drive, and came to the Esplanade along the Charles River.

Waltham played contentedly for some time on the swing, the jungle gym, and the slides (Sid joined him on the slides). Then, quite suddenly, the light wind changed direction and began to blow hard off the sea. The lightly falling flakes were replaced by a white wall of snow.

"Wally," said Sid, turning away from the wind, "I think we'd better start toward home."

Waltham, who was enjoying the excitement of the snow and wind, was very reluctant.

"Why don't we stop on Charles Street for a hot chocolate," suggested Sid. "We'll be more than half-way home by then."

Waltham cheerfully agreed to this suggestion, and they left the playground and walked along the Esplanade, bent against the wind and the stinging snow.

Sid put his flipper around Waltham as they crossed the footbridge. The wind was much stronger there. One gust threw them against the railing, and Waltham squealed.

"Blimey!" shouted Sid in alarm. They hurried down off the footbridge and were grateful to reach the relative shelter of the buildings along Charles Street.

They stepped into Miss Parson's Chocolate Shop with relief. There were a few tables, all empty. A small fire was glowing in a fireplace at one end. Along the back wall there was a long counter filled with chocolates, jellies, and sugary flowers.

They sat down next to the fire. It was very cozy.

"Well, here's Sid," said the tall pig who owned the shop. "And Waltham. You must want something hot," she said.

"Oh yes, hot chocolate please," said Waltham, who then turned his chair toward the fire.

"Make it two," said Sid, stretching his tail toward the fire. (He really would have preferred clam chowder, but the Chocolate Shop sold only sweets.)

Outside, the wind began to moan, and the snow beat against the window. Waltham and Sid sat silently in the coziness beside the fire. Miss Parsons set the hot chocolate in front of them and peered out the window.

"Looks pretty bad," she commented. "Not a soul on the street. Guess I'll close up early and get myself home."

"Better close soon," said Sid. "This blow promises to shut up Boston completely."

Just then a telephone rang sharply, and the proprietor went into the back to answer it.

"Mmmm, this is good," said Waltham, sipping his hot chocolate.

"Oh dear!" cried Miss Parsons, rushing into the room. "Mrs. Boylston's dog is out in the storm, and she's frantic, poor soul." She hastily put on boots and coat and rushed out into the wind.

"I'll be right back," she cried, "and then it'll be time to shut up."

"We'll just finish the hot chocolate and guard the candy until you come back," said Sid with a wave of his flipper.

Shortly after Miss Parsons went out, the wind began to howl outside and shake the doors and windows. Sid pulled his chair closer to the fire. Waltham moved closer, too.

"Better finish that hot chocolate," said Sid. "We're not far from home, but the wind's beginning to sound like we're rounding the Horn."

"Okay," said Waltham. "As soon as Miss Parsons comes back, we'll run for it. The hot chocolate will keep the wind from getting inside me."

They sat waiting for Miss Parsons, because they

couldn't just leave the shop unlocked and unattended. From time to time the wind gusted outside, and the building shook. They waited and waited. The fire burned lower. Sid began to get uneasy. "We really should be getting back home."

"While we're waiting," suggested Waltham, "maybe you'd better phone Mother or Nanny Trotter."

"Good idea, pal," said Sid, heaving himself up from in front of the fire.

"Phone's dead," announced Sid a few moments later. "I think we'd better head for home immediately, Miss Parsons or no Miss Parsons."

"Maybe she's lost in the snow," suggested Waltham.

"Let's hope she's found a safe refuge," said Sid. "It's time to batten the hatches," he added crisply, pointing to Waltham's hat and scarf.

"Keep a sharp eye," ordered Sid as he opened the front door tentatively. The room was immediately filled with a rush of snowflakes. This was followed by a huge drift of snow gushing into the room. "All hands!" yelled Sid, pushing hard against the door.

Waltham hesitated and then rushed up to help him. They just managed to push the door shut again.

"Come and help me clean up this mess, Wally," said Sid, picking up a dustpan.

Using a dustpan and a metal wastebasket, they managed to sweep up the snow before it melted all over the floor. Sid dumped it into the sink in the back room and washed it down the drain with hot water.

When Sid looked out the window of the shop, he saw that the parked cars were beginning to disappear under humps of snow, and Charles Street itself was unplowed.

"I'm afraid we'll have to stay put for the moment," said Sid. And suddenly the streetlights, which had just come on, went out.

"Oh gosh," said Waltham, "what are we going to do? The power is off." He was both a little afraid and a little excited about being stranded in the dark shop.

"We've got lots of wood," observed Sid. "That's lucky. Let's make a nice, bright fire to cheer us up. I'm sure someone will come for us as soon as it stops snowing so hard."

Sid and Waltham busied themselves making a large fire, and then Waltham sat on the rug in front of it. "Have two chocolate creams and a nap," said Sid, "and we'll be saved before you can say 'shiver my timbers.' "

Waltham slept fitfully for several hours while the wind howled around the shop. He would barely wake each time Sid got up to put more wood on the fire. And then he would snuggle against Sid's warm side and fall asleep again.

Waltham awoke with a start when daylight began to pour into the room. Snow was banked against the shop window, with light coming through the top pane only.

"I'm starving," said Waltham, looking up at Sid.

"Well, pal," said Sid, "maybe I can make some hot chocolate over the fire."

And soon enough he had a pot bubbling deliciously on a makeshift grate over the fire.

"Do you think Miss Parsons would mind if we ate some more sweets from the case?" asked Waltham, who was looking longingly at the glass case in back.

Sid laughed. "Now, under the circumstances," said Sid, "I don't see how she could object." Waltham scurried over and began filling a plate for both of them. "Cinnamon sticks," said Waltham, "candy canes, chocolate-covered almonds, lemon creams, peppermint patties, caramels, and gourmet jelly beans."

Waltham sat down happily and ate his breakfast. He didn't talk very much, but he made loud smacking noises; occasionally he would stop, smile to himself or at Sid, and then gobble down another piece of candy.

Sid ate too, although he found himself wishing for a few fish sticks.

Soon Waltham went back for seconds. Sid could hear him talking from behind the counter. "Chocolate creams, pecan clusters, fruit jellies."

Waltham bounced back to the table, his plate again heaped with sweets. "I never had a breakfast like this at home," he said, licking chocolate off his chin with his long pink tongue. "Maybe we should stay here awhile," he said, looking at the case full of candy.

"Romp! Romp! Romp!" The sound of someone pounding on the front door echoed through the shop.

Sid rushed to the door and, warning Wally to stand back, flung it open. Peering around Sid, Waltham could see his father standing in snowshoes. Behind him was Chester, the chauffeur. They had an old-fashioned sled piled with blankets. A cascade of snow entered the room with them.

"Well, you two look fine," said Livingston. "Miss Parsons tried to call you—she was stranded at her friend's—but the phone in the shop was dead. She got through to us just before the lights and phones went out on Beacon Hill, to tell us where you were. Your mother was frantic with worry. And Nanny Trotter was afraid you didn't get any dinner."

"I ate chocolates," said Waltham smugly. "And I slept in my clothes."

"I suppose it's all right under the circumstances," said Livingston. "We should be sure to leave some money," he added.

In short order they were dragged home and given a proper breakfast. (Sid got herring.)

Waltham was bundled off to a hot bath, where he told Nanny Trotter, "This was absolutely the best adventure I ever had in my life."

"Hmmph," said Nanny Trotter. "Stupid seal."

"We're not supposed to say stupid," said Waltham sleepily. Nanny tucked Waltham into bed, where he dreamed of other breakfasts—cereal replaced by chocolate creams, and toast (usually a favorite) displaced by a pile of pecan clusters (big ones).

Sid had a long, leisurely hot bath in his own tub. Then he too flopped into bed. There he dreamed of snowless tropical islands covered with bubbling hot tubs, one under each palm tree.

The White Cat's Story

In February, Livingston and Drusilla flew south for some sunshine, leaving Cook in charge of the house and Nanny Trotter in charge of Waltham.

On Sunday, Cook's day off, Nanny Trotter was called away quite suddenly by the sickness of a niece. She reluctantly left Sid to take care of Waltham.

Sid saw his chance. "Come on, kid," he said. "Do you think your folks would mind if I had a bath in their big tub? My bathtub is all very well, but the big de Swine bathtub is better."

"Well, they don't need it right now," said Waltham. "And if I bring my boats and you bring your boats, we can play shipwreck."

"Well, I've been in a few, and take my word, they're

not much fun, mate. Why don't you go up and get my big blue ball, and we'll pretend we're at the beach," said Sid.

Once the tub was full, Waltham and Sid installed themselves happily in either end. They began tossing the beach ball noisily.

"Yeow! This is fun," called Waltham as the ball whizzed back and forth.

"Meow! Meow!" came a plaintive voice. Sid dropped the ball and lifted his head out of the tub. Waltham looked over the edge, too.

There, sitting on the hamper, was a very thin white

cat. Her ribs were showing, and her whiskers had a distinct droop.

Sid draped a flipper over the edge of the tub and leaned out. "Miss, how did you get in here?"

"Ms.," she said promptly. She looked straight at Sid and switched her tail.

"Oh, sorry," he said. "Ms., how did you get in here?"

"There's a broken window in the basement," she said.

"Oh yes," said Sid, "I know all about that."

"Hey!" exclaimed Waltham. "I think I understand something now!"

"And . . . and," said the cat with a shiver, "it's wet and cold, and I'm terribly hungry."

"All hands on deck!" cried Sid, heaving himself up out of the tub. "Let's see what we can do. No one should go hungry."

"I'll help," said Waltham. He quickly began drying himself.

"Come along with us to the kitchen, Ms.," said Sid.

The white cat jumped off the hamper and followed him shakily down the stairs. She was very weak.

"What about a piece of cod and a bit of milk for starters?" asked Sid when they reached the kitchen.

"I'd be very much obliged," answered the cat, hurrying up to the fridge. "Then there's my family," she added in the same breath.

"Your family!" exclaimed Sid. "You've brought your family?"

"Yes," said the white cat. "I've hidden them in the basement, and they're all terribly hungry."

"Well, well," said Sid. "This must be remedied pronto. Come and introduce me to your family, Ms."

"This way," whispered the white cat, and she slipped through the half-open door to the basement.

Sid thumped down the stairs behind her, and Waltham followed. At the bottom she began mewing softly. Promptly they were surrounded by six large kittens, all mewing at once. They were all as thin as their mother. Some of them had trouble walking.

"Momma," cried a black-and-white kitten who was bolder than the others, "who's your friend with the big whiskers? Is that Papa?"

"Hush now," said the white cat. "This is a seal, and he has promised us some fish."

"Blimey!" exclaimed Sid, looking around at the

scrawny kittens. "This is terrible!" And bending down, he scooped up two of the weakest kittens in his flippers and headed for the stairs.

"Follow me, kittens," he called, and up the stairs he thumped, the other kittens and their momma trailing after.

During this scene in the basement, Waltham had stood there motionless and wide-eyed. He didn't know what to do; all that he had seen and heard was new to him.

Then, as the kittens marched after Sid, he noticed the black-and-white one slip on the bottom step and fall off. Waltham walked quickly over to the kitten and gently picked it up.

"Don't be afraid," he said, stroking the kitten. "We have lots of cod." And walking very slowly and carefully, he carried the kitten upstairs.

In the kitchen, Sid set out seven saucers for milk. "May I do that?" asked Waltham, and taking the milk carton from Sid, he filled each saucer carefully. Sid gave Ms. a large chunk of cod and set out smaller pieces for each of the kittens. When they had eaten their fill, the white cat came up to Sid and said, "I'm very grateful and especially so for the kittens."

The black-and-white kitten walked up to Waltham and rubbed its head on his leg. Waltham looked down and smiled.

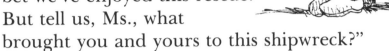

"Well," began Sid, "you can bet we've enjoyed this rescue. But tell us, Ms., what brought you and yours to this shipwreck?"

"It's a very simple story," said the white cat, "a story of fire and flight." They all sat around as she began her story. The kittens curled up around her, except for the black-and-white one, which crawled up on Waltham's lap. It began purring loudly.

And this is what Ms. told them: "My children—they were much smaller then—and I lived in Canton Warehouse on the waterfront. It was a well-kept building, and it was a happy life mousing and watching the sunrise over the sea. A wonderful place to raise children, especially since there were plenty of warm windowsills to lie upon.

"But one evil day, the people who owned the building sold it to a nasty pig named Jasper Rattle. He immediately began to neglect the building. It was no longer very warm, and Rattle wouldn't make repairs. Then the roof began to leak, and angry tenants moved out in droves.

"Finally, I decided to pluck up my courage and make a complaint to the owner in person. Jasper Rattle was very rude. He told me he didn't care if the building got run down and if I didn't like the situation I could always move.

"His parting words were designed to hurt my feelings. He turned to me with a sneer and said: 'I can always set out mouse traps, dear.'

"Can you imagine!" said the white cat, and she turned and gazed at Sid with wide eyes.

"Wow!" exclaimed Sid. "He really knows how to be nasty."

"Maybe he didn't really mean to be rude," said Waltham.

"He meant it, all right," said the white cat. "Two days later the whole place went up in smoke."

"Can you beat that!" said Sid.

"I never heard of such a thing," said Waltham.

"I'm sure the fire was set on purpose; it was no coincidence. Rattle probably wanted the insurance."

"How lucky you and the kittens escaped," said Sid.

"Fortunately, I was sitting on a window sill looking out at the full moon when I noticed two pigs come up to the building. They started pouring something out of a can. One sniff of the air told me it was kerosene. Without another thought I called my kittens together and led them down a back stairs and out into the cold.

"Looking back, I could see the building already beginning to flame and the two pigs running off into the shadows. We took refuge under an overturned rowboat and watched the building burn to the ground. The firemen couldn't save it.

"Since then we've been wandering from place to place. No one wanted to take in seven cats. It's been a struggle," she concluded, sighing deeply and looking at her thin kittens.

"That's a disgusting story!" exploded Sid. "People like that shouldn't be allowed to get away with wickedness." And he waddled up and down in agitation.

Waltham began to walk up and down, too. "That's just awful," he said. "Awful! I can't believe someone would do that on purpose."

The white cat and Sid looked at each other and smiled.

"That's the real world, young fellow," said Ms.

"Wally's led a very sheltered life here," explained Sid.

"Sid," said Waltham decisively, "you've got to do something."

"Hey, kid," said Sid, looking down at Waltham, "let's figure this out together."

"You mean there's something I can do?" Waltham asked.

"You're old enough to think," said Sid. "What we need is a plan for action."

"I'd like to help," said Waltham, his eyes shining. "Let's think."

Sid and Waltham

Take Action

Sid and Waltham paced up and down for some time. Sid would mutter something occasionally and clap his flippers together. Waltham would nod his head, and they would pace up and down again. Occasionally, Waltham would suggest something, and they would stop while Sid listened and nodded his head.

Finally, they stopped short and came up to the white cat. "Do you know where the owner of that building has his office?" asked Sid.

"Yes," replied the white cat. "That's where I visited him to complain. It's on India Street, near the waterfront."

"We should tell everyone what happened," said Waltham. "And we should tell the world about that mean pig," he added earnestly.

"Yes," she began, hesitantly, "but how can I, a mere white cat, do that?" As she said this, she placed a paw on her chest.

"If I can do it, you can," said Waltham. "We're all in this together."

"That's easy," said Sid. "We'll make signs, picket his office, create a commotion—people will notice. It'll be enjoyable, in fact."

"A wonderful idea," said the white cat, her ears perking up. "Maybe justice will be done!"

"I'll get some crayons and Magic Markers," said Waltham. "And paper!" He rushed upstairs.

When the materials were assembled, Sid immediately began to make a large sign for himself. He tacked it onto a stick so that he could hold it up with a flipper. His sign read:

ASK RATTLE WHO
BURNED CANTON WHARF
? ? ? ? ? ?
(WHO IS THE RASCAL?)

The kittens all crowded around while Waltham

made signs for them to wear. First he made a sign for Ms. It read simply:

UNHAPPY MOTHER

Then he made signs for all of the kittens. They read:

FIRE AND FLIGHT

SHAME!

HOME BURNED

A STARVING FAMILY

CRUELTY TO KITTENS

MEANNESS ON THE WATERFRONT

Finally Waltham made a sign for himself—a large sandwich-board type. It read on both sides:

WHAT RATT COLLECTED FIRE INSURANCE AND HOW DID HE SPEND THE BAD CASH?

The next morning, out of Cook's hearing, Sid called a taxi. When it arrived, the white cat and her family emerged from the broken window in the basement. Sid and Waltham came down the front steps, carrying signs.

The driver grumbled about so many in a taxi, but he drove them down to India Street anyway.

Twenty minutes later they were walking up and down in front of the granite building where Jasper Rattle had his office. Waltham's sandwich board was so big that it nearly hid him completely. Sid held his sign high, and the cats walked up and down stiffly.

"Do you think there'll be trouble?" asked Waltham. He was beginning to be anxious.

"We'll be okay, mate," said Sid, "As long as we stick together."

Sid had shrewdly called a newspaper and a TV station, and the TV crew had become very excited about a seal, a well-dressed piglet, and a family of cats picketing the offices of Jasper Rattle. The reporters and TV cameramen were already in place, and very quickly a crowd began to gather.

At nine-thirty a long black limousine pulled up, and Jasper Rattle, a very stout pig, climbed out. He was wearing a fur coat and carrying a black cane.

Immediately, flash bulbs began popping, and Jasper Rattle began roaring. "Get these stupid cats out of here!" he bellowed, looking at the cats wearing signs.

But already reporters were peppering him with questions, embarrassing questions. Jasper Rattle got very red in the face. "I'm not answering any of your questions," he said, his voice quavering. "I have nothing to hide," he said, ducking his head away from the whirring TV camera.

"Who burned Canton Warehouse, Rattle?" barked Sid, waving his sign in front of the same camera.

"Where did you come from?" shouted Rattle. "I'll see that you're sent back to the zoo, you whiskery snooper."

Sid made a rude noise, and the black-and-white kitten arched its back and spit and hissed.

"Watch out, rubber nose," screeched Rattle, "or I'll burn your pool!" And suddenly he struck out at Sid with his cane and kicked the black-and-white kitten.

"Nuisance!" shrieked Waltham, who had become very red in the face. "You're an awful nuisance," he cried repeatedly.

The crowd also became loudly indignant. "Beast!" shouted a small pig in a large flowered hat, and she suddenly began pummeling Rattle with her rolled-up umbrella.

Other spectators pushed in on Rattle and began pulling at his fur coat. "Nasty firecracker," cried a truck driver who pulled roughly back on Rattle's collar. Down he went with a roar.

Two policemen rushed up, rescued Rattle from the crowd, and pushed him into his limousine. It sped off with a squeal of tires.

Waltham bent down to comfort the black-and-white kitten, while a tall reporter stepped up to speak to Sid. "I'm an investigative journalist from WBBB-TV," he said. "What I've just seen and heard this morning convinces me that we'd better look into the whole story."

"Can you come to my office tomorrow?" asked the reporter, looking at the white cat.

"Yes indeed," said the white cat. "I will have plenty to say. It's a dark story," she added, "dark and dismal."

The small pig with the sturdy umbrella came up to the white cat and spoke softly. "My dear," she said, "I would like to offer you and your family a home. I live alone in a rather empty cottage, and the prospect of having such a nice family to sit with me in front of the fire would be very cheering."

"That is very kind of you," said the white cat, looking up at her. "Is there by any chance a warm windowsill?"

"Yes, my dear, I can offer you several warm windowsills and many saucers of milk."

"Saucers of milk!" cried all of the kittens in unison. "Oh yes, say yes, Momma."

"We'd be very much obliged," said the white cat, dropping her eyes modestly.

"Then why don't you come home with me right now," said the small pig. "I'm sure I can find pillows for you all."

Sid was very relieved by this outcome, but Waltham was crestfallen. He knew his mother would never approve of seven cats moving in with them, but he had become very attached to the black-and-white kitten.

"Well," he said, after thinking for a moment, "I'm going to ask Mother if the black-and-white kitten can come and visit me sometimes."

And so, with much mewing and some sniffling on both sides, Ms. and her family said good-bye. Sid and Waltham promised to come visit them in their new home very soon.

The two of them stood and watched the family walk up the street—the small pig, umbrella clutched tightly in hand, followed by seven cats with seven tails sticking straight up in the air.

"So all's well that ends well," said Sid, putting his sign into a trash barrel.

"And a piglet learns about sticking together," said Waltham, also chucking his sign into the barrel.

"Let's head for home, shipmate," said Sid, putting a flipper on Waltham's shoulder.

As they went up the street, Sid began singing a rollicking sea chantey, with Waltham joining in on the chorus.

Pull together boys,
Pull together boys,
Pull together boys,
And we'll all get home.

10

Sid Shows His Brass

There was great activity in the de Swine town house the first week of spring. Brass was polished, windows were washed, parquet floors were waxed and shined. The whole house, in fact, smelled of wax and honest soap.

But the shiniest of all, with a positively gleaming floor, was the de Swine's ballroom. Or rather, "the pavilion," as the family called the wing that had been added to the back of the house in the nineteenth century by Livingston's great-grandfather, to be used for his daugher's "coming out." It was there that the de Swines held a waltz evening every spring.

Waltham was very excited about the ball because

this year he had been told he could stay up for the party and watch the dancing. He kept asking Nanny Trotter how many more days.

On the appointed Saturday evening the guests began arriving in all their finery and gathering in the pavilion.

A large number of hired waiters were already scurrying around with trays of punch and tiny cookies. Sid was in charge, and he kept the waiters moving with his snappy enthusiasm.

At the end of the ballroom was a raised platform on which were set chairs and music stands for an orchestra. "It's not a ball without a live orchestra," said Livingston to a friend who questioned (as always) the expense.

The ballroom was becoming crowded with lady dancers in long dresses and gentlemen in black. Tall glass doors stood open to the garden because the evening was unusually warm for early spring.

Livingston looked at his watch. "And where is the orchestra, by the way?" he said aloud.

Just then Drusilla came bustling up. "The orchestra is not here," she said, gesturing to the place where they should have been.

Livingston, in sudden panic, bolted to the telephone.

Sid, who was scurrying around in his jaunty white bow tie, stopped abruptly when he heard Livingston's trembling voice. "Brockton, Massachusetts!" Livingston squealed. "But we're in *Boston*, Massachusetts!"

Behind him, Sid heard Drusilla shriek, and he turned in time to see her sag, fainting, into a convenient armchair. Sid rushed over and began fanning her pale face with his flipper.

"How can we proceed without live music?" wailed Livingston, who had dropped the phone in shock.

"Shocking incompetence!" blurted out Drusilla, who had opened her eyes.

"Does this mean there'll be no dancing?" asked

Waltham, his voice breaking. He looked at his pale mother and his shaking papa and then at Sid, who was still fanning Drusilla.

"Don't worry, kid," said Sid, patting Waltham, "I can find a way to make live music. Come with me."

He waddled over to two hired waiters and asked them to come upstairs with him to his room. Soon they reappeared on the stairs, the two waiters, Sid, and Waltham carefully carrying Sid's large trunk.

Sid directed them to carry it into the ballroom and set it down on the raised platform for musicians. He opened the trunk and began taking out a series of trumpets of different sizes. There were eight in all. Waltham, following Sid's directions, helped mount them on tripods.

"These horns belonged to my great-grandad," said Sid to Livingston, who had hurried up, all curiosity.

"Can you play waltzes on these horns?" asked Livingston, his voice brightening considerably.

"Sure, sport," said Sid. "I know a whale of a lot of waltzes, including many numbers by Strauss."

"Sid's going to play waltzes for us, Mother," announced Waltham, as his mother rushed up.

"Oh, Sidney," gasped Drusilla, "will you really provide live music?"

"You bet your best anchor," said Sid cheerily. "Only

thing is, I'll need something to keep my strength up.
. . ." His words trailed off.

"Punch! Punch!" cried Drusilla to a waiter who was
carrying a tray filled with overflowing glasses. "Bring
some punch for our musician!"

Sid drained off a glass rather quickly, smacked his
lips, snorted through his nose and moved behind the
horns. "Okay, folks," he called, clapping his flippers
together, "get ready for the first waltz."

The assembled guests looked up, surprised. They
hesitated, looking at each other.

Waltham walked up to his mother. "May I have
this dance?" he asked. Drusilla, looking at the standing
guests, smiled graciously and stepped out onto the
floor with her son.

Sid began to play the familiar melody of the Blue
Danube Waltz:

TAH TAH

BOOP BOOP

BOOP

TAH TAH

BOOP BOOP

He waddled quickly from one horn to the next in
order to play the melody. The sound at first was

rather jerky. At the same time there was an unmistakable waltz rhythm.

TAH TAH

BOOP BOOP

BOOP

TAH TAH

BOOP BOOP

Couples quickly began forming on the floor now. Soon the room was filled with turning forms and billowing skirts.

When he finished that waltz, Sid shifted to another, and already the playing was less jerky as he warmed to his task. That waltz finished, he began yet another.

Waltham whirled by, dancing now with his Aunt

Polly. His head came up to her stomach. "The music's wizard," he yelled over his shoulder. Sid could only roll his eyes in acknowledgment because he had to keep moving or there would be no music.

By the time the evening was over—many waltzes later—Sid had collapsed from exhaustion. Livingston directed four waiters to carry him up to bed. Drusilla, Livingston, and Waltham followed, all smiles. Waltham was carrying a glass of punch, in case.

"I can't tell you how grateful I am for this deliverance," said Drusilla, beaming at Sid. He smiled and smacked his lips.

Waltham handed him the punch. Sid took a sip, handed back the punch, and lay back on his pillow. "It was a real ball, Missus, and I had one too." And he barked his sealy laugh and closed his eyes with a sigh. Waltham set down the glass of punch, and they all tiptoed out, Waltham closing the door softly behind him.

The Urge North

Easter was late that year, and spring was farther advanced in Boston than usual. Clumps of daffodils and narcissuses had come into full bloom in the de Swine garden just in time for the Easter holiday. Drusilla decided to invite a group of Waltham's young cousins for an Easter egg hunt in the garden.

By ten in the morning the garden was full of squealing piglets hunting eggs. They swarmed everywhere: under bushes, in trees, and behind statues.

An hour later, when most of the eggs had been found, the squealing suddenly grew louder. A large black rabbit had emerged from the back gate of the garden.

It was Sid dressed in a black rabbit suit. He began passing out decorated chocolate eggs. "Have some rabbit's eggs, kids," he said jovially.

Waltham came up to him and looked closely. "Hi, Sid," he said. "After you're finished, would you play pig-in-the-middle with us? You can be first," he added.

"Sure, mate," said Sid chuckling. "But you'd better be on your toes."

The piglets rushed after Sid as he passed out eggs, and when his basket was empty, they stood around eating the eggs greedily.

"I saved an extra egg for you," whispered Sid to

Waltham. He stopped suddenly, looking up. The wind had freshened, and spare clouds scudded across the sky. "Strong smell of the sea," he said, sniffing the air. Sid's nose quivered rapidly, making him look even more rabbitlike.

"Nothing like that briny smell in the spring," he said, sighing. "The pull of the sea, you know," he said, looking down at Waltham. Waltham nodded and then, his egg finished, he ran up to his cousins.

"Let's play pig-in-the-middle," he shouted. "Sid's going to be 'it' first."

The piglets were very excited to have Sid in their game, and there was lots of squealing, together with some barks from Sid. But the noisiest and fastest of all was Waltham. "Watch me, Papa," he called energetically when Livingston stepped out on the terrace.

Nanny Trotter strode out behind Livingston and in a loud voice announced refreshments in the dining room. She looked suspiciously at Waltham's flushed face as he rushed up to the table with his cousins.

When the piglets had eaten every last cinnamon roll and gallons of hot chocolate had been diminished considerably, mothers and fathers began arriving to collect their children.

Waltham stood at the front door with his parents to say good-bye to his cousins. "See you tomorrow," he said to two cousins who were coming back the next day for a game of kickball on the Esplanade. "I've got a new ball!" he shouted after them.

Just as the last guests were making their way down the front steps, the phone rang, and a maid came to call Sid. She told him that a Captain Vierrha wished to speak to him. Drusilla and Livingston looked at each other, wondering what Sid was up to now.

When Sid reappeared, he said nothing.

"Lovely dress, Nanny Trotter," he said later, upon passing her in the hall. "Really becoming," he added.

"Well!" said Nanny Trotter, but there was a trace of warmth in her comment, alongside her astonishment.

At bedtime, Sid came to Waltham and read him several stories. Waltham surprised him by volunteer-

ing to read Sid a story about merry sailors on a clipper ship. Sid lay back on Waltham's pillow, enjoying every word of the lively sea story.

Waltham woke up the next morning at first light, as he often did. He propped himself up in bed and began reading his current favorite book, *Pigs at Sea.* He had only read a few pages when his door opened and Sid poked his head in.

"Up early, mate," he said.

"Sid!" said Waltham, "What's up?"

"Come to say goodbye," said Sid. "I'm on my way North."

"Do you mean you're leaving?" asked Waltham. His eyes had grown very large. "But why?"

"Oh I know it's very short notice but I just made up my mind. Every spring the sea calls this old sailor, and Cap'n Vierrha has offered to take me North when he sets out for the Grand Banks today. This way I won't have to swim in that bloomin' icy water."

"But I'll miss you a lot," said Waltham, his voice catching.

"I'm gonna miss you too, sport, but you know something, we're shipmates, like the two sides of a square knot. Wherever we go, nothing can pull that apart."

Waltham looked downcast.

"Say," said Sid, "I forgot to tell you—I'm leaving the horns for you—just so's you'll keep things cheerful."

"For me!" shouted Waltham. He smiled quickly and just as quickly looked sad. "But what'll I do without you?" he said.

"When I first saw you, I knew you were on a good heading," said Sid. "And you're still right on course, shipmate, all on your own rudder."

He reached out with his flippers and gave Waltham a hearty sailor's hug. Waltham, laughing, hugged back.

"Give this note to your parents at breakfast," said Sid. And with a cheery wave and a wink he hoisted a brand-new sea bag to his shoulder and was gone.

Waltham dutifully handed the note to his father at breakfast and watched solemnly while Livingston read it.

Dear Mr. and Mrs. de Swine:

   Sorry to leave in such a hurry but the tide doesn't wait for pig or seal and I'm heading North. I left my horns for Wally.

   Cheerio
   S. Seal.

Livingston's urgent questions to the Coast Guard and to a number of Gloucester fishing captains came to nothing. Sid was gone, and no one knew where. The whole household was wrapped in gloom: the maids quarreled, and Drusilla and Livingston snapped at each other.

Poor Waltham missed his friend Sid more than anyone. But when he was saddest, he remembered what Sid had told him and repeated it to himself. "He told me I was still right on course, and he called me shipmate!"

Waltham would smile then and square his shoul-

ders, because he especially liked being called shipmate. Still, it was a while before he could bring himself to open Sid's trunk.

Finally, on the first day in May, a day when windows were left open and fragrances from the garden drifted into the house, Waltham made an attempt to play the horns. He played many wrong notes, and he got out of breath from running up and down, but he also began to laugh.

A teacher was hired, and before long he was sounding the notes of some very simple waltz melodies. This made the whole household smile (even when there were wrong notes), and occasionally someone would be whirled around.

But Sid was still missed. Not a day went by without someone telling a funny story about him. Waltham was always ready to hear the stories and tell his own. But it was when Wally confided his ambitions that the whole household shook with amusement.

"When I grow up," said Waltham one morning to his father, "I'll grow big whiskers, go to sea, and learn to twirl a tray on my nose."

Livingston's eyes danced merrily for a moment, and then, unable to contain himself, he threw back his head and laughed heartily. "And what do we have here?" he asked when he finally caught his breath. "A small de Swine who wants to be a sailor!"

When he noted Waltham's expression, he bent down and put his arms around him. "Indeed," he said softly, "you could do worse, little Wally, much worse than being like Sid."

"Papa," said Waltham, suddenly, "do you want to hear me play my horns?"

"By all means," said Livingston promptly.

Waltham looked up and smiled at his father as they went slowly up the long curving stairs together.

A few moments later, the rather sweet sounds of the trumpets floated through the de Swine town house and drifted out the open windows, echoing against the stately walls and chimney pots of Beacon Hill.